7000150753

KU-614-822

University of the West of England
BRISTOL

EDUCATION
RESOURCES
CENTRE

This book should be returned by the last date stamped below.

UWE, BRISTOL B1084.03.01
Printing & Stationery Services

- 5 NOV 2002

- 4 DEC 2002

12. DEC 2003

24. NOV 2006

UWE BRISTOL
WITHDRAWN
LIBRARY SERVICES

WIZZIL

William Steig

WIZZIL

illustrated by
Quentin Blake

BLOOMSBURY
CHILDREN'S
BOOKS

For Jane and Bob —W.S.

First published in Great Britain in 2000 by Bloomsbury Publishing Plc
38 Soho Square, London, W1V 5DF

First published in America in 2000 by Farrar, Straus & Giroux Inc.,
New York

Text copyright © William Steig 2000
Illustrations copyright © Quentin Blake 2000
The moral right of the author and illustrator has been asserted

All rights reserved
No part of this publication may be reproduced or
transmitted by any means, electronic, mechanical, photocopying
or otherwise, without the prior permission of the publisher

A CIP catalogue record of this book is available from the British Library
ISBN 0 7475 5032 8

Printed in Singapore by Tien Wah Press

1 3 5 7 9 10 8 6 4 2

Wizzil the witch was busy biting her nails. "Beatrice," she said, "I'm bored stiff."

"Well, you've been perched in the same spot for so long this place is starting to stink," said the parrot. "Now, go and make somebody suffer!"

"But who?" said Wizzil. "And where?"

"Frimp Farm," yapped Beatrice. "It's a Frimpy family, all right. There's DeWitt Frimp, Fred Frimp, and Fred's wife, Florence Frimp."

Wizzil took her parrot's advice, turned herself into a common housefly, and zizzed on over to Frimp Farm to check it out incognito.

Snoozing and snoring, with a fly swatter in his fist, was DeWitt Frimp. He detested every breed of fly, especially *Musca domestica*. And since he wasn't up to milking cows anymore, he had plenty of time for swatting.

Wizzil landed on his bald head, and acting like a genuine fly, she sallied down his nose, crossed his cheek, and tickled his ear with her tiny feet. DeWitt sprang up, swishing his swatter wherever he could swish it, three times missing the witch by only a hair.

Resolved on revenge, Wizzil zoomed out the window, determined to cook up a really nasty plan. "Wizzil," she said to herself, "that bald-headed fuddy-duddy with his crazy swatter darn near did me in! He'll get what he deserves all right, and double-quick!"

Once she got home, Wizzil hurled her body onto her bed
and stared at the ceiling as if she dared it to try staring back.

Suddenly she got up and began pacing the floor in her snakeskin slippers. "Beatrice," said the witch, "listen. That old fogy keeps his swatter in his left hand, so he's a lefty.

“I’m going to turn myself into a left-handed work glove and make sure he wears me constantly. Then I’ll give him the works!”

“That’s the way, Wizzil,” Beatrice squawked. “Make him sizzle!”

Before sunrise the next day, Wizzil was down near the Frimp mailbox, skulking in the bushes. When the sun showed up, so did DeWitt, a fly swatter in his left hand and a letter in his right.

Presto! What had been a witch became a glove. After posting his letter, DeWitt spotted it.

"Frimp, my man, it's your lucky day!" he exclaimed, and he traipsed back home, pleased with his lucky find.

DeWitt took to wearing his new glove all the time, except when he washed or shaved or had to wind his watch or pick his nose. He wore it at breakfast, lunch, and dinner, as if that was normal behaviour.

Wizzil gave him time to get used to her, but then she got busy. And DeWitt soon found himself losing his war on the flies. He'd swing and he'd swat, and he'd hear the swatter swoosh, but Wizzil just jerked his arm a tad to this side or a tad to that side . . . missed again!

This made DeWitt dippy sometimes—he'd let out a war cry and chase the little devils all over the house, hitting everything in sight. Except flies.

“Are you all right, Dad?” Florence Frimp finally asked.

“I’m fine as wine,” DeWitt lied.

“Rubbish,” said Fred Frimp. “You’ve been acting nutty ever since you found that glove.”

“Nutty? If anyone around here’s nutty, it’s you. Anyway, I won’t stop wearing it.”

“Please, Dad,” said Florence. “Just take it off for one day and see what happens.”

“No way, and that’s that,” he said.

But they kept pestering him until the witch lost patience and decided to teach Fred and Florence to mind their own business. She began by giving them unbearable itches in unexpected places, and the harder they scratched, the more they itched.

At dinner that night she made their meatballs explode and their water spurt up like fountains.

And in the morning she made the whole house tremble
and shake so that the boards it was built with cried for help.

Making his sad way over the bridge that afternoon, having witnessed the weird things that were happening, DeWitt finally saw the light. Fred and Florence must be right. The glove had to be the culprit! He wrenched it from his wrist and flung it into the river.

Wizzil the glove began squirming and stretching and, right there in the water, began turning into the hateful hag she had always been.

And oh, how Wizzil hated getting wet (she hadn't had a bath since she was a helpless baby, and all she'd ever washed since then were her two horrid hands). She thrashed, gurgled, sputtered, and spat, and then she started to sink.

DeWitt stared in disbelief. But repulsive as Wizzil was, DeWitt couldn't bear to see a fellow creature drowning. He dived right in, and holding the disgusting witch in his arms, he started towing her ashore.

Halfway there, he was startled to see that this witch, instead of looking sinister, was blushing. *Blushing!* And smiling with gratitude into his wide-open eyes.

Wizzil had been so thoroughly cleansed by the crystal-clear water that all her vicious nastiness was whirled away downstream.

Instead of running for his life as soon as they hit the riverbank, DeWitt found himself hugging a surprisingly sweet old lady.

Needless to say, Wizzil and DeWitt fell completely in love, and wound up an old married couple who stayed together on the farm.

Wizzil was never bored again. Sometimes she and DeWitt even played cards with Fred and Florence, and Beatrice would help at their games.

"I guess I'll have to stay here with these humdrum humans," the parrot thought. "This'll be interesting."